A Flea Story

A Flea Story

by Leo Lionni

Alfred A. Knopf
New York

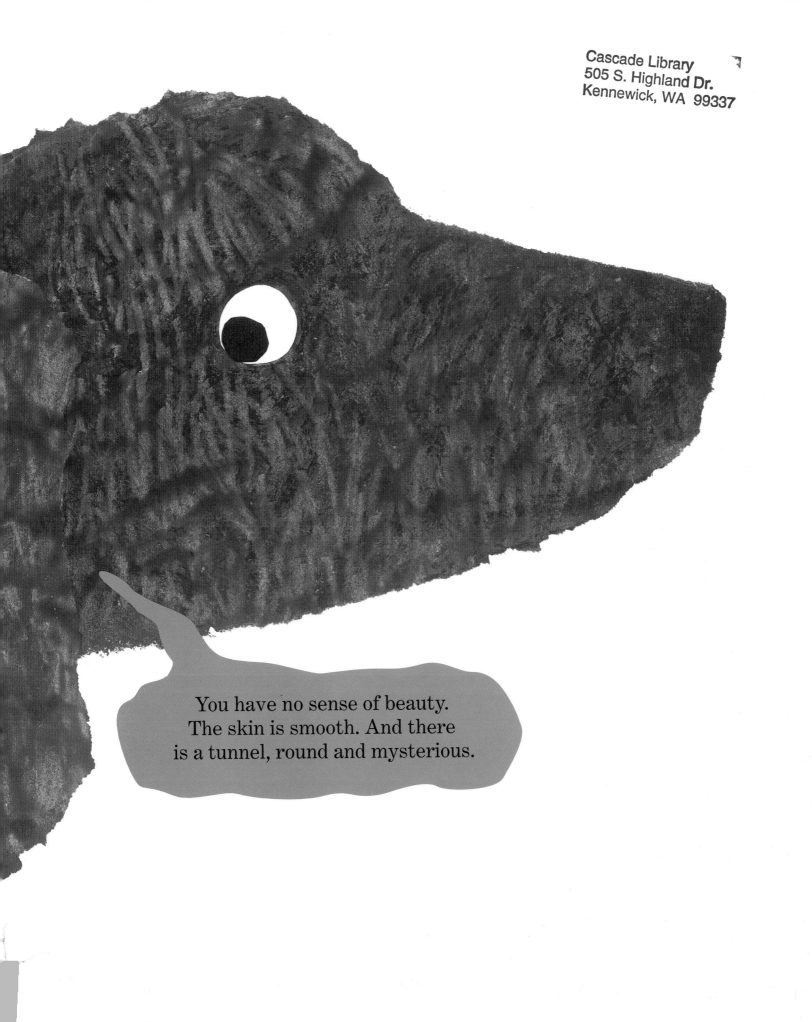

You have no sense of beauty.
The skin is smooth. And there
is a tunnel, round and mysterious.

I want to find out what life
is like on a porcupine.

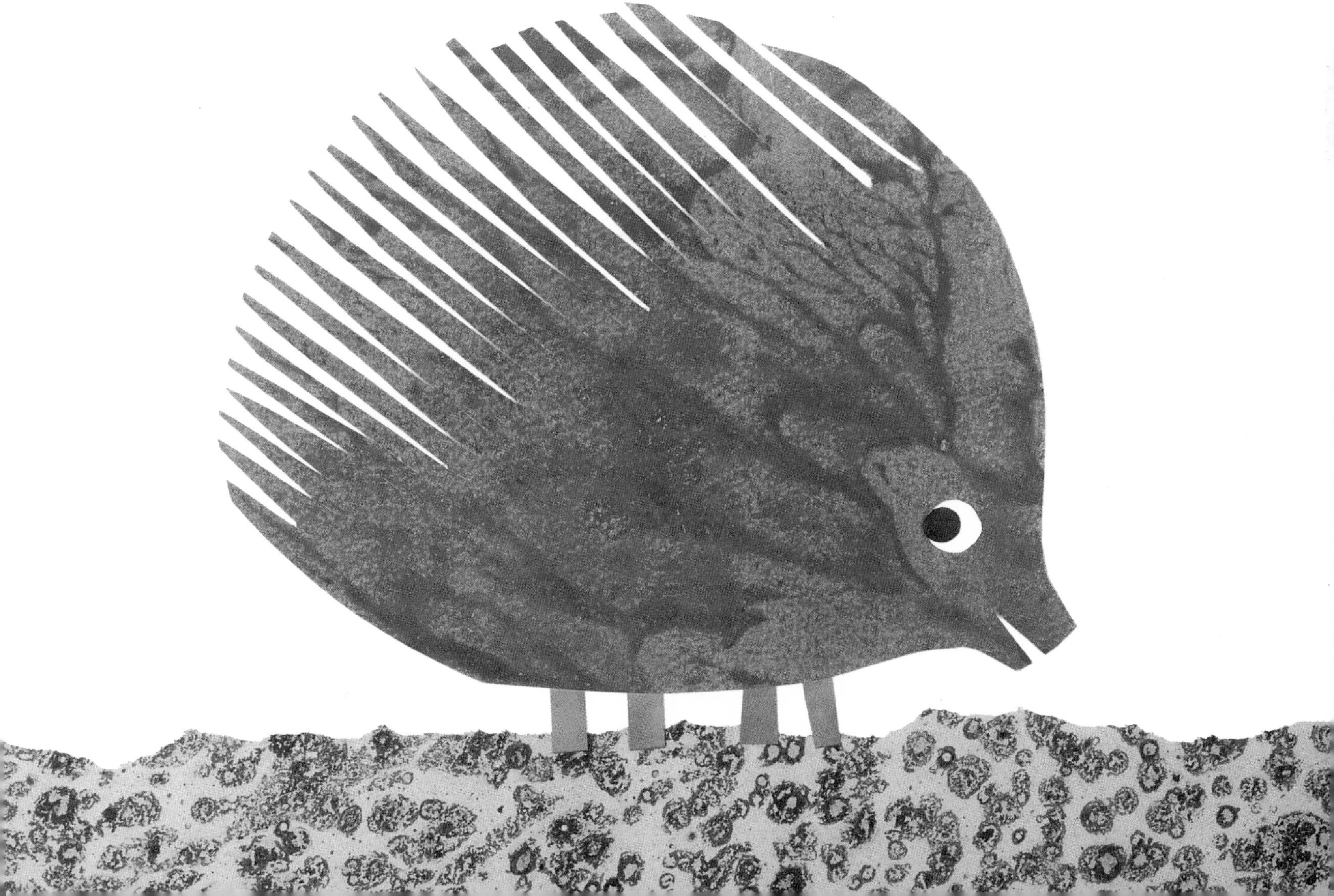

Everything here is hard and cold.
The quills are like a forest in winter.
Please let's go back to the dog.

Oh, you and your dog! Don't you enjoy
traveling and seeing new things? Look!
In that hole there is a mole!

Where are you? Help! I can't see a thing!

It is extraordinary! From here everything is almost as small as we are. A cow is no bigger than a bumblebee, and the woods are like flocks of sheep, huddled together in meadows. Someday I'll come back and tell you all about it. But will words be enough?

THIS IS A BORZOI BOOK PUBLISHED BY ALFRED A. KNOPF, INC.
Copyright © 1977 by Leo Lionni
All rights reserved under International and Pan-American Copyright Conventions.
Published in the United States by Alfred A. Knopf, Inc., New York, and simultaneously in Canada
by Random House of Canada Limited, Toronto. Distributed by Random House, Inc., New York.
Originally published as *A Flea Story: I Want to Stay Here! I Want to Go There!*
by Pantheon Books, a division of Random House, Inc., in 1977.
Manufactured in the United States of America   10 9 8 7 6 5 4 3 2 1

Library of Congress Cataloging-in-Publication Data: Lionni, Leo.
A flea story: I want to stay here! I want to go there!
SUMMARY: Two fleas, one who loves to travel and one who prefers staying home,
decide to go their separate ways. [1. Fleas—Fiction] I. Title.
PZ7.L66341ak [E] 77-4322 ISBN 0-394-83498-4 (trade) — ISBN 0-394-93498-9 (lib. bdg.)